21st Century Skills INNOVATION Library

Passenger Ships

by Judy Alter

INNOVATION IN TRANSPORTATION

Published in the United States of America by Cherry Lake Publishing
Ann Arbor, Michigan
www.cherrylakepublishing.com

Content Adviser: Amy C. Newman, Director, Forney Museum of Transportation

Design: The Design Lab

Photo Credits: Cover and page 3, ©Richard Goldberg, used under license from Shutterstock, Inc.; page 4, ©Steve Rosset, used under license from Shutterstock, Inc.; page 7, ©North Wind Picture Archives/Alamy; pages 9 and 27, ©Mary Evans Picture Library/Alamy; page 10, ©Eray Haciosmanoglu, used under license from Shutterstock, Inc.; pages 12 and 21, ©Classic Image/Alamy; page 15, ©Picture Contact/Alamy; page 16, ©alysta, used under license from Shutterstock, Inc.; page 17, ©abstrand, used under license from Shutterstock, Inc.; page 19, ©Ian Dagnall/Alamy; page 22, ©iStockphoto.com/pelicankate; page 24, ©GL Archive/Alamy; page 28, ©Ian Scott, used under license from Shutterstock, Inc.

Library of Congress Cataloging-in-Publication Data
Alter, Judy, 1938-
Passenger ships / by Judy Alter.
p. cm.—(Innovation in transportation)
Includes index.
ISBN-13: 978-1-60279-236-4
ISBN-10: 1-60279-236-4
1. Passenger ships—Juvenile literature. I. Title. II. Series.
VM381.A454 2009
387.2'432—dc22 2008002043

Cherry Lake Publishing would like to acknowledge the work of The Partnership for 21st Century Skills. Please visit www.21stcenturyskills.org *for more information.*

CONTENTS

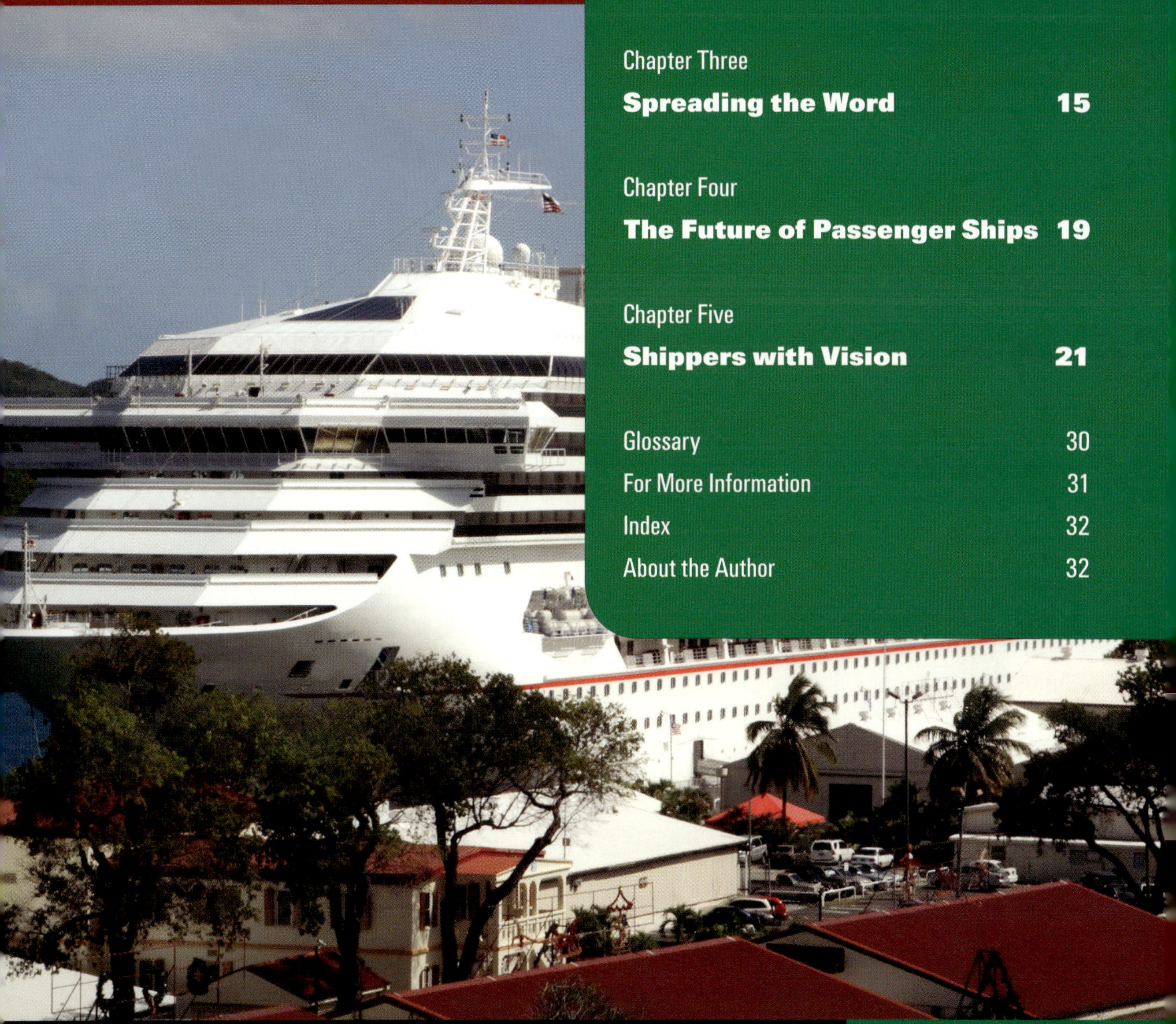

CHAPTER ONE

Travel by Water

Some ferries can carry hundreds of passengers and many cars.

Have you ever ridden a ferry across a small lake or to an island? Ferries can carry cars as well as passengers, so you can take your car with you. Or maybe your family has gone on a cruise on a huge ship with many activities. Those are passenger ships.

People have always wanted faster ships to reduce travel time. They want comfortable ships, too. Speed and comfort can help people enjoy traveling. Designers and shipbuilders use their imaginations and their skills to come up with bigger ships, better and fancier ships, and safer ships. Without people of imagination dedicated to travel by water, the passenger ships we know today would not exist.

People have been traveling on ships since ancient times. There were ships for exploring, ships for waging war, ships to move goods, and ships to bring people to new places. The *Mayflower* was a passenger ship. It brought 120 Pilgrims to North America in 1620 to find religious freedom. But it was a small, crowded ship made of wooden planks. Until the beginning of the 19th century, passengers who wanted to travel often searched for a cargo ship that was going where they wanted to go. When they found one, they asked if the captain had room for them.

For centuries, ships were propelled by manpower (often prisoners chained to one another as they rowed). Some ships waited for wind to fill their sails and push them along. Either way, wooden ships were dependent on the wind and weather. Weather became less of a factor with the invention of the **steam engine**. It made the development of modern passenger ships possible.

In 1769, in colonial America, an improved version of the steam engine was patented. In 1787, a man named John Fitch thought he could use an engine powered by steam to move boats through water. He conducted the

Learning & Innovation Skills

Sometimes innovation is not about being the first person to invent something. It can be about finding ways to use that invention. Robert Fulton is credited with identifying ways to use steamboats to make them a commercial success. In 1807, his ship, the *Clermont*, went from New York City to Albany, New York, a distance of 150 miles (241 kilometers), in 32 hours. (Today, such a trip by car would take about two and a half hours.) The steamboat's quick trip helped Fulton prove that steamboats were a profitable way to transport people and goods.

first successful trial of a steamboat. Later, he built a larger boat to carry passengers and freight between Burlington, New Jersey, and Philadelphia, Pennsylvania. Fitch received his first patent for a steamboat in 1791. By 1796, he had built four boats

Many other inventors were working with steam engines in Europe and America. Constant improvements were made in machinery and design. Success came slowly, so nations—particularly the United States and Great Britain—shared in the developing technology. At first, steamboats traveled on rivers and inland lakes. American steamships did not venture into the oceans. The English, however, sent steamships on **transatlantic** voyages. By the 1880s, railroads replaced steamboats for the transportation of cargo and mail. Passengers often preferred trains because they were faster than steam-powered vessels. The focus of passenger ships shifted to international travel.

An illustration of the *Clermont* shows the ship on its first voyage on the Hudson River in 1807.

American transatlantic ships were dependent on the weather. They could only travel when it was favorable. The first steamship to cross the Atlantic was a **paddle wheel steamer**. It traveled from Ireland to New York in

1838. Sir Samuel Cunard was the first to regularly send steamships across the Atlantic Ocean from British North America (present-day Canada). In 1843, the first steam-propeller-driven ship with an iron **hull**, SS *Great Britain*, crossed the ocean. But even early iron-hulled steamships carried both passengers and cargo, particularly mail.

Do you think of steamship travel as luxurious? For thousands of people who left Europe in the 1800s to live in the United States, the trip was long and difficult. They traveled in steerage, or third class, which was the cheapest way to travel. Steerage was the lowest level of travel available on a ship, after first class and second class. Passengers in steerage had cramped quarters, poor food, and little privacy. Many became ill during the trip, and some died. Usually first-class passengers made the trip in comfort on the upper decks. They enjoyed spacious cabins, fine food, and fresh air.

By 1900, there were several steamship **lines** in America—the American, the Red Star, the Atlantic Transport, the White Star, the Leyland, and the Dominion. In 1902, these lines banded together to form the International Navigation Company. The new company was financed by famous Wall Street banker J. Pierpont Morgan. Morgan invested in railroads, banking, and insurance companies. He headed the banking company of J. P. Morgan. He was often called a tough businessman,

An advertisement features the White Star company's RMS *Homeric*, which sailed between Southampton, England, and New York City during the 1920s and 1930s.

interested only in power and making money. But Morgan was a smart businessman. Signs of his success were his luxurious mansions and yachts.

The International Navigation Company (which eventually changed its name to the International Mercantile Marine Company) scheduled ship departures. One company controlling all passenger lines could regulate rates and schedules. One luxury ship owned by the company departed for Europe each week. The shipping **conglomerate** was one of Morgan's least successful ventures. It was dissolved during the **Great Depression** of the 1930s.

Airplanes travel faster than ships. They can also reach more destinations than ships.

By the 1960s, airplanes were replacing passenger ships as the preferred way to travel. Passengers decided they would rather fly between distant cities (for example, New York and London) than take a week to travel there one way by ship.

The popularity of air travel meant shipowners had to think of new ways to attract passengers. Ship companies began to add extra attractions to their ships. Soon the trip itself became the reason for sailing, rather than just sailing as a way to get from one place to another. The cruise industry was born.

Learning & Innovation Skills

Passengers aboard today's luxury cruise ships have much more comfortable sailing experiences than those aboard ships of the 1800s and early 1900s. But the journeys of those early passengers, especially those in steerage, are not forgotten. Today, passenger lists from those ships are valuable to researchers trying to trace family histories. The lists tell who came to America, from what country, and when. Many families search passenger lists on the Internet to find their ancestors. If you travel aboard a passenger ship, you'll be listed as a passenger. Perhaps one of your descendants will see your name on that list.

Shipowners didn't have family history in mind when they started keeping passenger lists. Can you think of some reasons why it is important to have a list of the people traveling on a ship?

CHAPTER TWO

Improving Safety

Perhaps the most famous shipwreck ever was that of the RMS *Titanic*. The largest ship of its time, it was also one of the most luxurious. Passengers on her maiden (first) voyage from England to the United States included

The *Titanic* was built in Belfast, Ireland, and was more than 880 feet (270 meters) long.

some of the most famous and richest people in the world. Many immigrants were also traveling in steerage. The *Titanic* was called "practically unsinkable." On the night of April 14, 1912, however, the ship struck an iceberg and sank about 3 hours later. It had 20 lifeboats on board, but there weren't enough for all the passengers and crew. About 1,500 people died. The sinking of the *Titanic* was the worst peacetime **maritime** disaster in history to that point.

The sinking of the *Titanic* is an event that jump-started innovations in passenger ship safety. Soon after the tragedy, an International Conference on the Safety of Life at Sea was formed. The leaders of 14 nations signed a set of new passenger safety guidelines. Iceboats patrolled the ships' routes for icebergs. Iceboat crews warned ship captains in time for the ships to change course. Wireless communication technology was used. Captains also took notes on icebergs they saw. Most ship lines moved their routes 40 miles (64 km) to the south to avoid icebergs.

Shipbuilders put their best minds to work on improving safety. They added a double hull to the ships, with space between the two hulls. With this new design, if the outer hull was penetrated by an iceberg, the ship would not sink as quickly as the *Titanic* did. There would be more time to save passengers and crews.

Some of the new safety rules seem simple to us today. Shipowners are now required to provide a life vest and a place in a raft or lifeboat for every passenger and crew member. It was decided that passengers should be educated on safety. They should be shown where to go for a lifeboat, how to get to deck quickly, and how to put on their life vests. Today, all international ships require their passengers to go through safety drills before or as they set sail. This helps prepare everyone for a possible disaster and prevent future tragedies.

Life & Career Skills

The leaders of passenger ship lines have set high standards for safety and expect their employees to meet those standards. Today's high-speed data technology helps captains and their crews meet these expectations. The same technology used in air traffic control systems for airplanes is used with passenger ships. The use of radar and computers allows electronic route planning. Ship collisions can be avoided by signaling well in advance when ships are in the same area. Computers can also send messages when ships are in distress so that help can arrive. Ships also have equipment that helps them detect submarines or icebergs. All of these innovations keep passengers and crews safe.

CHAPTER THREE

Spreading the Word

As air travel became easier and more popular, passenger ship companies saw a decrease in business. The owners of passenger ships needed to find new ways to attract customers. They began offering more cruises—trips for pleasure and sightseeing instead of just to get to the destination.

Shipowners knew they needed to do more to attract travelers. One of the first new additions to cruise

A costumed dancer performs during a show on a cruise line. Staged performances were one of the first forms of entertainment offered on cruise ships.

Cruise ships feature many extras, such as swimming pools and water slides.

travel was elaborate shows. They hired dancers, singers, comedians, and other entertainers to stage these shows for passengers.

Then companies began to build ships especially for cruises. Previously, cruise ships were just unused passenger ships. There was nothing special about them. Shipping company leaders decided they could attract more customers by building ships with more features. They added swimming pools, shuffleboard courts, restaurants, and even libraries. Today, the biggest and fanciest ships have many extras. It isn't unusual to find ships with spas, gyms, running tracks, rock-climbing walls, multiple restaurants, and many shops.

At first, cruises went to the Caribbean, Alaska, and Mexico. But shipowners knew they could attract more people with new and different destinations. Today, several hundred ships sail all over the world. Some ships even sail to the Arctic and to Antarctica.

A running track rings the upper deck of a cruise ship.

21st Century Content

In the age of international terrorism, cruise lines have to reassure travelers that their ships will not be targeted by terrorists. In 1985, Palestinian terrorists hijacked an Italian cruise ship, the *Achille Lauro*. Incidents like this one are uncommon, however. Cruise ships are generally safe because they are a controlled environment. This means that people cannot come and go constantly, the way shoppers do at a mall, for example. Today, passengers, crews, and their baggage go through security screening much like that done at airports. Cruise ships are also subject to U.S. Coast Guard regulations, and a 100-yard (91 meter) safety zone is maintained around ships at all times. This safety zone keeps ships safe from being approached or surrounded by vessels that might do them harm. Adapting to 21st century challenges has helped the cruise industry become more popular than ever.

After the terrorist attacks on the United States on September 11, 2001, many people were afraid to travel by airplane. The cruise industry, however, blossomed because of innovative marketing. Cruise lines advertised their ships as floating hotels and entertainment centers. Traditionally, ships departed from Florida or Puerto Rico. But in the 2000s, they began to depart from a variety of coastal locations throughout the United States. People did not have to take airplanes to exciting destinations. They could go on cruises instead.

CHAPTER FOUR

The Future of Passenger Ships

The cruise industry is flourishing in the 21st century. Companies are building more ships, larger ships, and more complex ships all the time. The future will depend, in part, on continued safety. Cruise ships compete in a world that is crowded with vacation destinations such as Walt Disney World Resort. Ship designers and engineers will continue to improve their ships and

Cruise ships compete for customers with resorts such as Walt Disney World Resort in Orlando, Florida. The resorts feature amusement parks, water parks, golf courses, hotels, and restaurants.

attract famous entertainers to interest more passengers.

In 2008, Celebrity Cruises announced that it would be adding a lawn to one of its new ships. The ½-acre live-grass lawn will allow passengers to practice their golf putting. Or they can simply take off their shoes and feel the soft grass between their toes.

While some cruise lines are building ever-bigger ships, others are turning their attention to creating smaller, more personalized travel opportunities. They seek to provide new travel experiences to passengers by offering river cruises in Europe, Russia, Egypt, North America, Southeast Asia, and China. These passenger ships are much smaller, holding no more than 250 people. They move slowly along narrow waterways, but offer scenic beauty and historical sites.

21st Century Content

Some cruise lines increase interest in their business by offering vacations that appeal to people with specific interests. For example, Silverseas offers a cruise featuring an executive chef from *Bon Appetit*, a gourmet food magazine. On the 110-day World Cruise 2008, celebrity chef Cat Cora presented Greek-inspired specialties while passengers crossed the Aegean Sea. The cruise also took passengers through the Caribbean, the Pacific, the Far East, and the Mediterranean for a once-in-a-lifetime trip around the world.

CHAPTER FIVE

Shippers with Vision

Many people have contributed to making passenger ships the luxury vessels we know today. Here are just a few of the innovators who helped pave the way for the modern cruise ship industry.

Born in Pennsylvania, Robert Fulton was one of several inventors who worked to develop steam-powered boats.

Robert Fulton

Robert Fulton may not have invented the steamship, but he made steamboats a commercial success on rivers and lakes in the United States.

Today, some steamboats are replicas, or reproductions. Others are old boats that have been restored.

While studying art in Europe, he became interested in steam engines. He met Robert R. Livingston, who was also interested in steam power. They partnered to build a steamboat. It sank in the Seine River in Paris, France. They decided to return to America, where Fulton would build a boat and Livingston would fund the project. The *Clermont* had a steam engine in the hull and paddle wheels on either side.

Livingston had money and political power. He secured the exclusive right to run steamboats on New York rivers and on the lower Mississippi River. Fulton's second ship, the *New Orleans*, launched on the Ohio River in 1811. It made regular runs between New Orleans, Louisiana, and Natchez, Mississippi. The *New Orleans* often ran aground on sandbars in the tributaries of the Mississippi River. Fulton believed the route needed a boat with a flatter hull that didn't sit so low in the water. That would keep it afloat.

Fulton eventually withdrew from the steamboat business, but he and Livingston had realized the importance of river waterways and the part they played in opening lands to the western United States. By 1816, passenger and freight ships were well established on the Mississippi River. Fulton and Livingston also opened the Hudson River to shipping: in 1819, there were 8 steamboats on that river; in 1840, there were more than 100.

Isambard Kingdom Brunel

Isambard Kingdom Brunel was one of the great shipbuilders of the early 1800s. Born in Portsmouth, England, he was the son of a French engineer. He spent his early years engineering railroads. In his twenties, he built about 1,200 miles (1,900 km) of railroad between the English cities of London and Bristol. Then he built railroad lines in Ireland, Italy, and India. His accomplishments included the first tunnel under a river, as well as viaducts and bridges.

Brunel's SS *Great Western*, built in 1837, was the first iron-hulled steamship in regular transatlantic service.

Isambard Kingdom Brunel's engineering projects included tunnels, bridges, and steamships. He also redesigned several docks in Great Britain.

SS *Great Eastern*, built in 1859, was the largest ship at that time, with room for 4,000 passengers.

Ships were not his main interest. But his biggest contribution to the industry was to make the large **screw-driven**, all-metal steamship a reality. He was ahead of his time. Industrial conditions in America and Europe did not make transatlantic travel practical until later.

Samuel Cunard

Samuel Cunard established a steamship line that continues today. He began the business with his father to develop trade in timber and West Indian goods. After the War of 1812, he established the North American Royal Mail Steam Packet Company, known thereafter as the Cunard line. He began with four small, wooden, steam-paddle-driven ships. The first steamship, SS *Britannia*, sailed in 1840, with Cunard himself at the helm.

He knew that one of the difficulties of ocean travel was its irregular schedule. Ships left when the weather was favorable. But when there was a storm at sea, ships could be delayed for days or even weeks. He was determined to have the first regular service across the Atlantic Ocean. Passengers could plan their schedules, arrange hotel accommodations, and schedule meetings. His first iron ship, SS *Persia*, sailed in 1855.

J. Bruce Ismay

J. Bruce Ismay may be the most tragic figure in shipping. Ismay came from a shipping family in England. After travel and an apprenticeship, he became the New York agent for the White Star Line, founded by his father. In 1891, he returned to England and became a partner in the firm of Ismay, Imrie & Company. By 1899, he was head of the business. When the firm became a part of the International Mercantile Marine Company, he served a term as president of the shipping conglomerate.

Ismay wanted to attract steerage passengers, who were the biggest source of his income. At the time, thousands of immigrants were coming to the United States every year. He planned the largest ship yet, with maximum steerage space for immigrants. He believed that space, not speed, was the key to attracting immigrant travelers. The upper decks would have luxury accommodations for wealthy passengers. He commissioned shipbuilders in Belfast to build the *Titanic*.

Ismay always went on the maiden voyage of his ships, and he was on the *Titanic* the night it sank. He was among the survivors, and some newspapers blamed him for the tragedy. They wrote that he urged the ship's captain to go too fast. This is false. Ismay knew that having a ship arrive ahead of schedule caused many problems at the dock with refueling and taking on fresh

A White Star Line postcard features an illustration of the *Titanic*, one of the most luxurious ships of its time.

water and supplies. It was also a problem for travelers with hotel reservations.

Ismay was also accused of being a coward for taking a place in a lifeboat and, later, for resigning from his company rather than facing the public. He was able to

Today, passenger ships have more safety and emergency equipment than earlier ships did.

document that he had helped women and children into lifeboats. When the last boat was about to leave, he called loudly for any passengers; none responded on the deck where he was. He took a seat in the boat at the last minute. But the tragedy of the *Titanic* followed Ismay for the rest of his life.

Life & Career Skills

Newspapers at the time of the *Titanic* disaster portrayed J. Bruce Ismay as a coward who took a place on a lifeboat that could have been given to a woman or child. This is not the truth. Ismay didn't board the lifeboat until he was sure that there were no women or children on the deck. Still, many believed that he should have stayed aboard the *Titanic* and gone down with the ship. They said it would have been the honorable thing to do.

What do you think? If you were Ismay, what would you have done? Why?

Glossary

conglomerate (kuhn-GLAH-muhr-it) a number of small businesses or organizations banded together for their mutual advancement; in this case, a number of shipping lines

descendants (di-SEN-duhnts) the members of your family who live after you

Great Depression (GRAYT di-PRESH-uhn) a worldwide period of economic difficulty, with high unemployment, much poverty, low prices on goods, and a general freezing of the economy; in the United States, the effects were increased by the Dust Bowl, a drought that ruined crops, making less produce available

hull (HUHL) the frame or body of a ship

lines (LINES) companies that own and operate ships that travel over specific routes

maritime (MA-ruh-time) having to do with the sea

paddle wheel steamer (PAD-uhl-WEEL STEE-mur) a steam-powered boat that is also propelled by a wheel with paddles around its circumference

screw-driven (SKROO-DRIV-in) a ship with a propeller instead of paddles

steam engine (STEEM EN-juhn) an engine that uses the energy of steam and converts it to mechanical energy

transatlantic (tran-suht-LAN-tik) crossing the Atlantic Ocean

For More Information

BOOKS

Jenkins, Martin and Brian Sanders (illustrator). *Titanic*. Cambridge, MA: Candlewick Press, 2007.

Mega Book of Ships: Discover the Most Amazing Ships on Earth! London: Chrysalis Children's Books, 2003.

Wilkinson, Philip. *The World of Ships*. Boston: Kingfisher/Houghton Mifflin, 2005.

WEB SITES

CNN.com—The 411 for Young First-Time Cruisers
www.cnn.com/2008/TRAVEL/traveltips/03/25/young.cruisers/index.html
For cruise travel tips for kids

NASA—Cruise Ships, Kids, and Science
http://www.nasa.gov/audience/foreducators/5-8/features/F_GLOBE_Cruise_Ships.html
Information about a NASA program for gathering scientific data while on a cruise ship

Index

About the Author

Judy Alter has written numerous books for young readers on a wide variety of topics. She values the education she gets from researching topics such as passenger ships, because she's never been on a ship herself, except for a ferryboat. The mother of four and grandmother of seven, she lives landlocked in Fort Worth, Texas, with her dog, Scooby, and her cat, Wynona.